Raintree is an imprint of Capstone Global Library Limited, a company incorporated in England and Wales having its registered office at 264 Banbury Road, Oxford, OX2 7DY – Registered company number: 6695582

www.raintree.co.uk
myorders@raintree.co.uk

Editor: Michelle Bisson
Designer: Hilary Wacholz

ISBN 978 1 4747 2843 0 (paperback)

British Library Cataloguing in Publication Data
A full catalogue record for this book is available from the British Library.

Printed and bound in India.

Worry WARRIORS

Edgy Estella Enjoys the Sleepover Party

by Marne Ventura
illustrated by Leo Trinidad

raintree

a Capstone company — publishers for children

CONTENTS

ALL ABOUT THE
Worry
WARRIORS

My name is Estella Garcia. I live with Mum, Dad, my sisters Sofia and Isabella, and my brother Carlos in a city near the sea. I am nine years old. I have dance lessons. I love to watch movies and TV shows with princesses, mermaids, dancing, and singing. I have long, wavy brown hair and brown eyes. I hope to be a cheerleader when I'm at secondary school and a movie star when I grow up.

Luckily, my three absolute best friends ever live on my street. We've gone to school together since pre-school. And it turns out we all worry about something. And then we work together to help one another out.

Nellie likes reading, writing, word games, and school. That's excellent because she wants to be a writer when she grows up.

Jake loves to read, like Nellie does. He is good at maths, science and computers. He wants to be a scientist one day. He's saving up for a robot racing car.

Adam is awesome at sport, art and building projects. He has dyslexia. That means he learns to read, write and spell differently from most kids.

Three summers ago, when we were six, we were making hula-hoop bubbles in Nellie's back garden. We were barefoot, running around on the wet grass. I almost stepped on a bee. I totally freaked out! I ran into Nellie's house and wouldn't come back to play until Adam scooped up the bee with a plastic cup and put it into the bin. And put the lid on. Tight.

I felt silly being so afraid of a tiny bee. But I had just watched a TV nature show about bees. They're super-creepy when you see them up close. They're really hairy, and their faces look like monsters.

I guess Nellie didn't want me to feel silly alone, because she told us that she was afraid of the dark at bedtime.

She imagined scary stuff, like that her toys might come to life and attack her, or that monsters might be hiding in her wardrobe.

Then Adam said he gets scared walking across the bridge that goes over the dual carriageway. He holds on super-tight to his mum's hand and tries not to look down.

Jake said he was afraid to wade into the sea because he could feel slimy stuff with his feet. What if he stepped on a poisonous jellyfish?

After we told each other our worries, we felt better. We didn't make fun of each other, like some kids would. And, we realized, if all of us had secret worries, maybe they weren't silly at all.

That's when Nellie had the best idea ever. She said we should form a club. First we would tell each other our worries. Then together we would fight them, like knights and warrior princesses in shining armour.

And that's how we became the Worry Warriors.

Chapter 1

★

You've got mail!

It's a Saturday morning in January. My little sisters and I have just finished our class at the Beach Street School of Dance. We're waiting for Mum to pick us up.

"I can't wait for our dance recital," I tell my friend Grace. "I'm so excited!"

Grace Lee is in my dance class, and also in my class at school. She has straight, black shoulder-length hair with a fringe. She's wearing a pale pink leotard and tights, like my sisters and me.

"I know," says Grace. "We get to wear tiaras! Like in *The Princess Diaries*."

"That's my favourite princess movie," I say. "I've watched it so many times."

Grace plops down next to me on the wooden bench in the foyer of the dance studio. It's a cool, sunny day, and through the window, I see people walking dogs and pushing babies in pushchairs along Beach Street. My seven-year-old sister Isabella and my five-year-old sister Sofia are sitting next to me, swinging their feet back and forth under the bench.

"It's so cool how she finds out she's heir to the throne and she didn't even know her grandma was a queen." Grace swings her feet under the bench, too. "Do you think that could really happen?" Grace asks.

"Sure! I have aunts and uncles and grandparents who live in Mexico. Ever since I watched the princess movie, I wonder if one of them might turn up one day to tell me I'm a princess."

"Wow," Grace says. "I have lots of relatives I've never met in China. Do you think that could happen to me, too?"

"Maybe," I say. "It would be fun to get princess lessons, like the girl in the movie. But one thing I wonder about – do you think princesses have to be good at maths?"

"Probably," Grace shrugs. "Or I guess they could have a maths assistant."

"I need a maths assistant," I say. "I didn't expect Ms Anderson to give us a surprise test yesterday."

"I know," Grace nods. "I missed five problems because I didn't finish in time."

"I missed even more!" I say. "If I have enough time I can count out the answers, but I can't do times tables fast."

I haven't shown Mum and Dad the maths test yet. They're not going to like it when they see I did badly.

Grace's mum pulls her car up to the curb and Grace jumps up. "Bye, Estella. See you in school on Monday."

Grace's best friend since pre-school is Ashley, and my best friend since pre-school is Nellie. This is the first year that we've been in different classes from our best friends. It has been really hard to get used to. Ashley and Nellie are in the other year 5 class – Mr Meaney's. I really miss being in the same class as Nellie, but we still get to spend time together before and after school and at lunch and break.

It's not enough, but it's better than nothing.

As soon as Grace's car pulls away, Mum steers our people carrier into the same space and waves to me. My three-year-old brother Carlos looks out from his car seat behind Mum.

I take Isabella and Sofia's hands as we walk to the car.

"How was your class?" Mum asks as she gets out to help Sofia buckle up.

"There's going to be a recital," I say.

"We get to wear tutus," says Isabella.

"And crowns," says Sofia.

"She means tiaras," I tell Mum. I hand her the letter that tells about the recital.

She reads it. "What fun!"

As Mum starts the car and pulls out onto Beach Street, Sofia asks, "Mum, can we watch the princess movie after we eat lunch?"

"Maybe after dinner," she says. "You have chores to do.

And do you have homework? We didn't ask last night."

I don't answer. My stomach flip-flops when I think about showing my maths test to her and Dad.

"I've finished my homework already," says Isabella.

"Where's Dad?" I ask. He usually comes with Mum to pick us up. Sometimes we go out for lunch after our dance class.

"He had to work," says Mum. "He's close to a deadline on a big project."

Dad is an architect. He designs houses.

We reach our house, and Mum pulls the car into the garage. "Will you pick up the post, Estella?"

I bend down and pick up three bills and two magazines from the door mat. Then I see a square envelope with my name on it! It's pale pink, and there's a silver star stuck on the flap. What could it be? I never get post.

As I run into the kitchen to show Mum, I think about *The Princess Diaries*. What if this is the letter that tells me I'm a long-lost heir to the throne? I would definitely not want to miss that!

"Mum! I've got post!" I hold up the pink envelope.

Sofia, Isabella, and Carlos come over to look.

"What could it be?" asks Mum as she puts avocado slices on our wraps.

I separate the flap gently, so it doesn't make a rip in the pretty envelope.

My sisters and brother all talk at once.

"Just open it," says Isabella.

"What does it say?" asks Sofia.

"I wanna see," says Carlos.

When I finally get the envelope open, I pull out a pink card with silver sparkles on one side. On the other side, there's a party invitation. "Please join us for Brittany's 10th Birthday Art Party." There's a cartoon of a girl with long brown hair like Brittany, holding a paintbrush and palette.

"Mum, can I go?" I ask, pleading.

Brittany is new to Sea View Primary School this year. She's not in my class – she's in the other year 5 class, with Nellie. I don't know her very well, but she seems nice. We were both princesses in the Winter Extravaganza. I'm excited to be invited to her party.

"When is it?" asks Mum as she dishes up bowls of hot soup.

I look at the date on the invitation. "The weekend after next."

Isabella takes the card from me. "It's so pretty. Oh, look, Estella. It's a sleepover."

I read the card more closely. Yikes. The party starts at 5:00 p.m. on Saturday night and ends at 9:30 a.m. on Sunday morning. I'm supposed to bring my sleeping bag, pyjamas, and toothbrush. Isabella's right. It's a sleepover.

Even though I'm nine, I've never been on a sleepover before. I'm excited but also scared.

Chapter 2

★

Yes, on one condition

"Mum, you met Brittany's parents on the first day of term," I remind her as we sit down to lunch.

Mum and Dad have a rule that before I can go over to someone's house, they have to meet their parents.

"That's right," says Mum. "They seem like a nice family. I remember Brittany's mother is an artist, and her father teaches at the university with Nellie's mother."

"So, can I go?" I ask.

Half of me wants to go, and the other half feels worried about the sleepover. Last year Grace had a birthday sleepover party, and the year before Ashley had one. But their invitations said "Sleepover Optional." That meant you could go home at bedtime. That's what Nellie and I did.

But this invitation doesn't say that. If everyone else is sleeping over and I want to go home at bedtime, I might look like a baby.

"Can we go, too?" ask Sofia and Isabella.

"I wanna go," says Carlos.

Mum laughs. "This party is for year 5 children. You'll get invited to parties for friends your age."

To me, Mum says, "What do you think, Estella? Are you ready for a sleepover?"

I know Mum is thinking about Grace and Ashley's parties. Nellie and I took our sleeping bags and pyjamas to both of those parties. But when it was time for bed, we decided we wanted to go home.

"Yes," I tell Mum. But inside, I'm not so sure.

"Well," says Mum. "We'll talk it over with Dad at dinnertime."

After lunch I clean my room and do my spellings homework, and Mum says I can call Nellie and invite her to come over.

When the doorbell rings, Isabella, Sofia, and Carlos all run to the door.

"Nellie!" they call out as I swing the door open. "Yay!" they say, when they see Adam and Jake beside Nellie.

"Hi," I say to Adam and Jake. "What's up?"

"Can you come to the park with us?" Adam says.

"Thanks," I say, "but I just called Nellie to come over. We need to talk about this sleepover we've been invited to. It's a girl thing."

"Oh, okay," Jake says. He looks a little disappointed.

"Jake, Adam, look at this." Carlos holds up his toy truck.

"Cool," say Jake and Adam.

Sofia grabs Nellie by the hand.

"Look at me, Nellie," she says, twirling around.

"Me, too," Carlos tries to twirl and falls over.

"Good dancers." Nellie claps.

"Well," Jake and Adam say, "if you get bored, come and join us."

"Thanks," I say. Nellie and I wave goodbye and go into my room to talk.

"Did you get your invitation to Brittany's party?" asks Nellie, when we sit down.

"Yes, I love getting post! And the invitations are so cute," I reply.

"Brittany's mum made her post them, since she's only inviting five girls," Nellie explains. "It wouldn't be right to hand them out at school."

"Do you know who else is invited?" I ask.

"Grace and Ashley, you and me, and Alexis," says Nellie.

"Alexis Sweet?" I ask. Alexis doesn't have a best friend. She doesn't usually get invited to birthday parties. She's good at school and talks to teachers politely, but she's not very good at being nice to people her own age.

"Brittany lives next door to Alexis. So Brittany's mum said it would be rude not to invite her," says Nellie. "Are you sleeping over? I'm not sure what to do," Nellie adds just as the door opens. Isabella, Sofia, and Carlos all come in.

"Nellie, look at this." Sofia has the letter about the dance recital.

"Nice," says Nellie. "Are you going to wear a tiara?"

"Yes." Sofia twirls around the room.

Carlos gets down on his hands and knees and makes truck noises as he rolls his truck along the floor.

"Nellie, thanks for the book," Isabella returns a book that Nellie lent her.

"Everybody out," I say. "Nellie and I are trying to talk about Brittany's party."

"We'll be quiet," Isabella and Sofia say. "We want to stay. It's our room, too."

"Okay," I say, "but find something to do, so we can talk." Nellie and I sit cross-legged on my bed.

"I'm worried about the sleepover part," I say.

"I had fun staying with Grandma and Grandpa for a week last summer," says Nellie. "I think I may be ready for a sleepover."

"You're lucky to get to practise with grandparents," I say. "I've never done a sleepover, not even with relatives. They're all too far away!"

"Now that we're almost ten, it seems babyish not to sleep over," says Nellie.

"I have another problem," I tell her.

"What is it?"

I pull my maths test from my desk drawer to show her. "Ms Anderson keeps giving us surprise tests," I say. "I can't remember my times tables fast enough. We have to finish the test in five minutes."

"Uh-oh," Nellie takes the page from me and looks at it. "You got the right answers on the ones you did. It's just that you left most of them blank."

"Mum and Dad are going to make me practise more. I haven't shown it to them yet," I say.

"Does Mr Meaney give timed maths tests?" I ask Nellie.

"He does," says Nellie. "But I've moved out of that maths group. Now I'm in a group with Brittany, and we're doing fractions and decimals."

"You're so good at maths," I tell Nellie. "I guess Brittany is, too." I don't tell her that it seems like Brittany is good at everything. And that it sort of bothers me.

Nellie says, "Maybe when you show your mum and dad the maths test, you can tell them we've been practising. That way, they'll know you're trying to do better."

"Good idea." I get out my flashcards and draughts game. Time to get some help from my best friend.

Isabella, Sofia, Carlos, and I sit on the floor. Nellie holds up a multiplication card for me, subtraction for Isabella, easy addition for Sofia, and number cards for Carlos. For every correct answer, we get to move our counter forward one square.

We play until Mum knocks on the door. "Nellie's mother

just called for her to go home. And Dad will be here soon, too. Time to get ready for dinner."

I walk Nellie to the door.

"Good luck telling your parents about the maths test," she whispers as she leaves.

Soon we're sitting around the dinner table with Dad.

"How was your day?" Dad pours milk into our glasses.

"Estella's been invited to a sleepover," says Isabella.

"The invitation is pink and sparkly," says Sofia.

"We played numbers with Nellie," says Carlos.

"Whose party?" Dad takes a plate of chicken fajitas from Mum.

"Brittany," I say. "You and Mum met her parents on the first day of school, remember?"

"What's this about numbers?" Mum sets a basket of tortillas on the table

"Well," I say, "I've been meaning to tell you about my maths test."

"It was a surprise," says Sofia.

"And Estella only had five minutes," says Isabella.

Mum and Dad are both looking at me now.

I pull the test out of my pocket and hand it to Dad. "I didn't do so well. But Nellie and I practised all afternoon."

Mum looks at the test. "Estella! You should have shown this to us yesterday."

"What do you think about this, Estella?" Dad hands the paper back to me.

"I need to practise. A lot," I say.

"I'll tell you what," says Dad. "Let's make a deal. You can go to Brittany's party on one condition. You need to spend at least thirty minutes a day practising those times tables. Deal?" Dad holds up his hand, and I slap it to show I agree.

Inside I feel all mixed up. Is it worth spending all that time on maths practice, so I can go to a party that might turn out to be a big catastrophe?

Chapter 3

★

Bookworms

"Dad says I can go to Brittany's party on one condition," I tell Nellie, Adam, and Jake as we walk to school together on Monday morning. "I have to practise my times tables for thirty minutes every day."

"That's not so bad," Jake pushes his glasses up. "I can come over after school and help if you want. I've got a fun practice game on my tablet."

"That's what Isabella told me," I say. "She helped me with flash cards yesterday. I think she knows more than *I* do."

"I'll come, too," Adam says as he hops over a crack in the pavement. "I'm not doing so well on those surprise tests either."

"Okay," I say. "I hope we don't have a test today. I'm not ready yet."

We get to school and put our rucksacks by our classrooms. Jake heads to the computer room, Adam joins a football game, and Nellie and I walk around the edge of the playground.

"I just finished *Ella Enchanted*. It was the best book," Nellie shows me the cover. "It's sort of like *Cinderella*," she says.

"I saw that movie," I say. "It was good."

"You should try the book," Nellie holds it out to me.

"If I saw the movie, I don't need to read the book," I say.

Nellie laughs. "But it might be fun, silly."

The bell rings, and we say goodbye until break time.

***

"Hi!" Grace is already in the line for class. "Do you think we'll have a maths test this morning?"

"I hope not." I tell her about my one condition for going to Brittany's party.

Luckily, we don't have a maths test, and at morning break Grace and I walk out to the playground together.

We find Nellie, Ashley, and Brittany out on the grass.

"I know," Ashley is saying. "*Ella Enchanted* is my all-time favourite book."

"The next one in the series is super-good, too," says Brittany. "That author writes a lot of princess books."

"I'd rather watch the princess movies than read the books," says Grace.

I agree with Grace, but I don't say anything. I feel grumpy. Why is Nellie having so much fun talking about books with Brittany and Ashley? Usually I'm the one she has fun with.

***

Alexis walks up. "Are you talking about Brittany's art party? When I have a party, it's going to be a glamour spa theme. We'll do facials and paint our nails and do our hair."

"That sounds awesome," I say.

Nellie looks surprised . . . or mad. I'm not sure which, but I ignore her.

"Very awesome," says Grace.

Ashley says, "I'm going to have a bookworm theme for my party."

"What a good idea," Nellie and Brittany say together.

Grace and I look at each other, a little left out.

"Maybe I'll have a ballerina party," says Grace.

"That sounds fun," I say.

"Not for me," says Alexis. "I'm not into ballet."

"I'm not really, either," says Nellie, "But – "

The bell rings before Nellie finishes. Ashley, Grace, Brittany, and Alexis walk towards the classrooms, Nellie waits for me.

"What were you going to say about Grace's ballerina party?" I ask.

"Just that a birthday party is supposed to show what the birthday girl likes," she explains. "You don't have to be into ballet to go to a ballerina party."

"Oh – right." I'm a bit relieved. I was afraid Nellie was going to say she didn't think a ballerina party was cool.

"Are you definitely sleeping over at Brittany's party?" I ask as we walk.

"Yes," she smiles. "It'll be fun!"

"I keep thinking about how we decided to call our parents to come and get us last year at Grace's party," I say.

"We were only eight then," says Nellie.

"And the year before, at Ashley's."

"We were only seven then," says Nellie.

"I guess I'm the only one who feels nervous about sleeping over."

"You know what you need?" asks Nellie.

I nod and smile. "I do! Emergency Worry Warriors Meeting. ASAP!"

Chapter 4

★

Emergency meeting

The next day after school, Nellie, Adam, Jake, and I meet in Nellie's tree house in her back garden. That's where we always have our Worry Warriors meetings.

The tree house is cute. It's made of wood. Nellie's dad built it for Nellie's big brother, Henry, when he was little. Henry started secondary school this year. He doesn't mind if we use it. Last summer we painted the door red and planted red flowers in the window boxes.

To start the meeting, we put on the Viking helmets that we got at the after-Halloween sale a couple of years ago. We know we're a bit old for this, but it's tradition.

Then we raise our hands and yell, "Don't worry, be happy!" That's our Worry Warriors battle cry.

It's how we always start meetings.

"I hereby call this meeting to order," says Nellie. "Let's start by saying what worries us about sleepovers. And birthday parties."

We settle into our beanbag chairs.

"And remember," I say. "Nobody is allowed to say someone's worry is stupid."

"Right," Adam agrees. "What happens in the tree house, stays in the tree house."

"No making fun or laughing," Jake adds.

I go first. "I'm worried about it being an art party," I say. "I'm not good at art. You guys have seen my drawings. I can barely make a stick figure."

"You're good at decorating your room," says Nellie. "And figuring out which clothes to wear together. And making up costumes. Those are all art."

"But I think Brittany's going to make us draw or paint. I can't do that," I whine.

"I'll help you practise," offers Adam. "I have an amazing drawing book."

"I can find out from Brittany what the projects are," says Nellie. "Then you'll know what to practise."

"Okay, thanks! But I have another worry," I continue. "You know how Sofia and Isabella and I share a bedroom? We tell each other stories until we fall asleep. If Carlos can't get to sleep, he comes and sleeps in our room, too. What if I can't get to sleep without them?"

"I'll be there," says Nellie.

"That's true." I smile. "That does make me feel better. I have another worry, though. I know it's supposed to be fun to stay up past your bedtime, but I get really tired and grumpy when I do. This is embarrassing, but the tiniest thing will make me cry when I'm sleepy."

"Just go to bed early the night before," says Jake. "Or take a nap the afternoon of the party."

"That's a good idea. But what if I fail another maths test and Mum and Dad don't let me go at all?" I say.

"They said you could go if you practise, right?" says Adam. "So, practise every day. Besides, I bet you'll do much better on the next test."

Jake and Nellie nod in agreement.

"Jake and Adam, do you guys worry about birthday parties and sleepovers?" I ask.

"My friend from the University for Kids computer class had a tent sleepover in his back garden," says Jake. "It was okay, but we heard animals moving around outside. That was kind of creepy."

Adam says, "My friend from football had a camping party last summer, and we slept out in the woods in tents. There were no streetlights or building lights. I woke up in the middle of the night, and it was so dark I couldn't see anything. It was pretty scary. So, you might want to take a torch, just in case."

"My sister says I snore," adds Jake. "So I worry about that at sleepovers. I don't even know if it's true, since I'm asleep, but it still bothers me."

"I dribble," says Adam. "My mum says it's normal, but I think it's embarrassing."

"Now I'm really worried," I say. "Maybe we should just go to the party and not sleep over, Nellie."

"You can do it!" Nellie, Jake, and Adam say together. "What's the worst thing that could happen?"

"I could cry, dribble, snore, do the worst art project, not be able to get to sleep, and the other girls could think I'm a baby because I'm the only girl in year 5 who has never slept over," I say. "Or, it could be spooky dark and animals could be creeping around outside."

"I have an idea," says Nellie. "You can do a practice sleepover at my house this weekend!"

"Wow, great idea," I say.

As we adjourn the meeting, I feel better about the sleepover. I'm lucky to have good friends who help me out. And I think sleeping over is a princess skill I need to have. But there's one worry I didn't say out loud at the meeting: Why do I have so many worries and Nellie doesn't? Is she growing up faster than I am? Or is she more comfortable with sleeping over at Brittany's because they're becoming good friends? Without me?

All of that worries me. A lot.

Dance party

On Wednesday after school, Jake, Adam, and Nellie come to my house. Jake brings his maths practice game, and Adam brings art stuff and his drawing book.

"Look at my teapot dance," Sofia says. "I'm going to do this at the recital."

We all watch, and then clap when she's finished.

"Adam," Carlos says, pulling on his hand, "let me show you my castle. I made it from blocks!"

"Cool!" Adam says.

"Nellie," Isabella says, "look at the book I got from the library. It's a mystery. You will love it."

Finally my little brother and sisters have finished, and

Jake shows me the maths practice app on his computer. It flashes multiplication problems and the sooner you click on the right answer, the more stars you get. If you get stuck on a problem, it shows a grid with all the times tables so you can see the right answer. We play for a while and I get a score of three stars out of five. Not bad!

Isabella wants a turn to play the game with Jake, so Adam shows me his drawing book. He has some sketchpads, and he gives one each to me, Nellie, and Sofia. There's a step-by-step lesson for how to draw a car in the book. We all get to work.

Drawing is fun. I forget about my worries as I follow the directions in the book. First I draw the body, then wheels, then windows. My drawing doesn't look great, but I can tell it's a car.

"Look!" says Sofia in a little while.

I look up from my drawing. Sofia's car looks about the same as mine. Maybe a little better. And she's five years old! It's embarrassing, but I can't say that. Instead I say, "It's nice, Sofia."

"Oh, by the way, Estella," says Nellie. "I talked to Brittany about the party and she says we're doing an art project where we paint monarch butterflies on pillowcases. It sounds super fun."

Nellie picks up some coloured pencils from Adam's art box and starts to put flowers on her car. It looks fantastic.

I look over at Jake and Isabella, using the maths game on Jake's tablet.

"Four out of five stars," Jake tells Isabella.

"Estella! I'm learning my times tables too," Isabella says.

Why is everyone better at everything than me? Even my younger sisters? I put my pencil down and cross my arms over my chest. I feel like exploding. Instead, I take a deep breath in and then let it out.

Sofia comes over and pulls on my arm. "Estella, you look sad," she says. "Do the teapot dance with me."

I frown. I don't feel like doing the teapot dance with Sofia.

Carlos pushes his truck up onto my toe and makes it go up my foot. *"Chug-a-chug-a-chug."*

I look at Nellie. She lifts her eyebrows, which means, *What's wrong?*

"I can't draw a butterfly," I tell her. "I can't even draw a car! And my little sister is faster at multiplication than I am."

Nellie puts her pencil down. "But you're a good dancer. And you're very princess-like. If you ever find out you're heir to the throne, you'll be ready."

I laugh and feel a little better. I watch Sofia as she does her teapot dance.

"Oh, whatever." I make one arm into a handle and one into a spout and dance the teapot dance with Sofia.

"I'm a little teapot, short and stout," sings Carlos as he joins us.

Nellie, Jake, and Adam do it, too. "Here is my handle, here is my spout."

We all do the teapot dance together.

"Let's do crazy-dancing," says Sofia.

Jake plays some fast music on his tablet and we all crazy-dance.

"This feels good," I tell Nellie as we twirl around.

"You're a good dancer," says Nellie. "You look so graceful when you twirl. I think I look funny when I dance."

I think Nellie's right, but I don't say so. Instead I say, "I guess everybody has some things that they're good at."

"Adam's a good dancer," says Isabella.

I look at Adam, crazy-dancing. He does look good. "You're right!" I say.

"Me, not so much." Jake laughs as he waves his arms around. "But it's fun, anyway."

I twirl, then do my best arabesque. "Ta-da!" I call, as I leap across the room. Gracefully.

This would be a good time for my long-last royal relatives to come and get me. Before the sleepover party.

Chapter 6

★

Spooky stories

At school the next day, I worry that we'll have a test. I know I'll do better than last week. With more time to practise, I might even get them all right. *Please, Ms Anderson*, I think, every time she starts a new activity, *no maths test yet.*

I take my flashcards with me to practise at morning break. At lunch break, Nellie and I walk around the edge of the playground and talk.

"I got Brittany's birthday present – the next book in our favourite mystery series," says Nellie. "And I found the cutest wrapping paper. It has bookworms on it."

"Mum helped me pick out some gifts," I say. "A pad of watercolour paper and a paint set. I hope she likes them."

Ashley and Grace walk up together.

"Brittany says we're going to watch a movie," says Nellie. "And have pizza and birthday cake."

"I wonder if it will be a scary movie?" asks Grace. "That's usually what we watch at sleepovers."

"My brother is always telling me spooky stories," Ashley says.

"I watched a *scary* movie last weekend." Grace leans in as she talks in a low, spooky voice. "These kids were on their way home from school and a big storm came up. They thought there might be a thunderstorm, so they went into this old, broken-down barn, even though it was dark and about to fall down."

"Um – " I want to yell, "I do not like spooky stories or scary movies." I know Nellie doesn't either. But she isn't speaking up, and I don't want to look like a baby. I have such a hard time getting scary things out of my mind once I hear them. They pop up when I'm trying to go to sleep at night and scare me over and over again!

I'm saved when the bell rings. Grace stops telling her story, and we all start to walk towards class together. I drop behind the other girls and Nellie stays with me.

"Do you think Brittany likes scary movies?" I ask, when it's just the two of us.

"I really hope not," Nellie frowns. "Do you think Grace and Ashley could be right? Maybe everyone tells spooky stories and watches scary movies at sleepovers. What if we're the only ones who don't want to?"

Finally, I'm not the only one who is worried about the sleepover! Oddly, that makes me feel a bit better.

"Maybe we should tell Brittany we're coming for the party but we're not sleeping over," I tell Nellie.

"Or, *maybe*, we should practise listening to spooky stories and watching scary movies when we have our practice sleepover!" Nellie holds her hands up, like it's a brilliant idea.

"Maybe," I say. But what I'm really thinking is, *MAYBE NOT!*

Chapter 7

★

Practice makes perfect

Mum and Nellie's mum agree that we can have a practice sleepover at Nellie's on Saturday night.

On Friday Ms Anderson gives us a maths test. I pass!

"See, Estella?" Mum hugs me when I show her my mark after school. "Practice makes perfect."

"Not perfect yet," I say. "But way better than my last test."

On Saturday afternoon, I go to my room to pack for Nellie's. Isabella, Sofia, and Carlos watch while I put my clothes in my overnight bag.

"It'll be weird, not having you here tonight," Isabella says with a frown.

"I know. I'll miss you," I say. "Maybe we can call each other at bedtime."

"Good idea!" Isabella jumps up. "I'm going to go and ask Mum."

Mum thinks it's a great idea, and she says if I promise to be careful, I can take her mobile phone to Nellie's.

I put the phone, my pyjamas, pillow, and my toothbrush inside my sleeping bag.

"Here." Sofia hands me my old, ragged, soft ballerina doll. When I make my bed in the morning, I sit her on my pillow. She has a pink leotard and tights and a pink tutu. And black ballet shoes. Her name is Katrina. I've had her since I was three.

"Okay, put her in," I say. I let Sofia stuff her into my sleeping bag.

Dad walks me over to Nellie's when he gets home from work. He carries my rolled-up sleeping bag.

"Good job on your maths test." He puts his hand on my shoulder as we walk. "I'm proud of you."

"Thanks, Dad," I say. He makes me feel better.

"Keep practising," he says. "It's important to know your times tables."

"I will. Were you good at your times tables when you were in year 5?"

"Terrible," Dad smiles. "I didn't want to practise, same as you. But my dad made me do it, and now I use maths every day to design buildings. And it's fun."

"But I want to be a movie star," I say. "Why do I need to know my times tables?"

"So you can count your money!" says Dad.

We both laugh.

Nellie opens her front door and waves. "Hi, Mr Garcia. Hi, Estella."

Dad comes in to say hello to Nellie's parents, and Nellie and I go into her bedroom.

Nellie already has her sleeping bag set up on the floor. I lay mine out next to hers. There's a big lump where my pillow and pyjamas are. I wonder what that is, but I'm too excited to look right now.

"Mum and Dad wouldn't let me rent a scary movie." Nellie is searching around on her bookshelf. "In fact, they say they're sure Brittany's parents won't let her show a scary movie at the party."

"Oh – " I'm about to say that's good news.

"So," Nellie turns around with a book in her hand. "I have another idea. I got a collection of spooky stories from the library that we can read together."

I can't believe Nellie is suddenly interested in scary stuff. She never was before.

"Did you ask Brittany if she's planning scary movies and spooky stories?" I ask.

"No," Nellie shakes her head. "I don't want her to think I'm afraid. So, let's practise, just in case."

"Okay," I say. I'd rather have a dance party or watch the teenage mermaid show, but maybe Nellie's right. Maybe we do have to practise.

Nellie opens the book and starts to read about a nine-year-old boy who's good at carving animals out of wood. He carves a statue of a monkey and puts it on his windowsill. That night there's a big storm. Every time the lightning flashes and lights up his bedroom, the monkey is in a different position!

Nellie stops reading and looks at me with big eyes. "Are you getting scared?"

I nod. "Thunder and lightning always scare me. And I know statues can't move, but that's spooky, too!"

"Maybe we should take a break," Nellie says and stuffs the book under her sleeping bag.

"Nellie, Estella!" Nellie's big sister, Lucy, opens the door. "Mum says, wash your hands for dinner."

"Hooray!" We follow Lucy into the kitchen. I'm starving!

I've known the Davis family all my life, and I've eaten dinner with them before, but knowing I'm going to stay here all night makes me feel shy. I think about my family sitting down to dinner at home without me.

We take our places around the table and Nellie's mother puts a big bowl of spaghetti and meatballs, a basket of garlic bread, and a bowl of salad on the table. At our house, Mum dishes up our plates for us. At Nellie's, we pass the food around and dish up our own. I hope I'm taking the right amount, and that I don't spill anything.

After dinner, we help clear the dishes and Nellie and I watch an episode of the mermaid show. Three teenage girls turn into mermaids if they get wet during a full moon. One of them works at a sea life park. In this episode, she has to save a baby dolphin who lost its mother. The other girls help. Nobody can know that the girls are mermaids, so they have to tend to the dolphin secretly.

"It would be awesome to have some special secret like that," I tell Nellie.

"Like a superpower," agrees Nellie. "I think that would be really cool."

Then Mrs Davis says it's time to put on our pyjamas and brush our teeth. We put on the matching pyjamas we

got when we went shopping together during the Christmas holidays. The trousers have red and white stripes, and the long-sleeved T-shirt tops are red. Then we sit on top of our sleeping bags and play card games for a while.

"Should I read more of the spooky story?" asks Nellie.

I'm feeling sleepy. I hadn't slept well last night because I was nervous about sleeping over at Nellie's. I rub my eyes and lean my back against Nellie's bed. "I guess so. Are you getting sleepy? It is kind of late. Or do you want to watch another mermaid episode? Or part of the princess movie?"

"I've seen that princess movie so many times." Nellie yawns. "I'm a little tired of it."

Now I feel grumpy. How could anyone be tired of the princess movie?

"And," adds Nellie, "I've used up my TV time for today, so my parents will say no."

This makes me super-cross. First of all, I bet her mum and dad would let us watch more TV if we asked. And why does Nellie always want to read instead of watching TV?

I suddenly wish I were home in my own room, with my own family.

Nellie pulls the book out, opens it, and starts to read again. In the story, raindrops are hitting the window like crazy. Thunder crashes. But this time, when lightning strikes and lights up the bedroom, the monkey is gone! The boy hears a funny scratching sound on the floor . . .

This story is making me scared, and I'm so tired. I think I'm going to cry. I'm about to tell Nellie to stop, when a loud ringing sound makes us both scream and jump up.

"What *is* that?" Nellie's eyes are huge, and her voice sounds shaky. "Where is that noise coming from?"

Then I remember, I put Mum's mobile phone in my sleeping bag!

I reach in, pull it out, and answer it.

"Estella?" I smile when I hear my sister's voice on the line.

"Hi, Isabella!" I say happily.

"I just wanted to say good night," she says.

"Good night!" I say back. "Are Sofia and Carlos there?"

"I'll turn the speaker on," says Isabella.

"Hi, Estella," I hear Mum, Dad, Sofia, and Carlos.

"I miss you," says Carlos.

"I'll be home tomorrow," I tell him.

"Say goodnight to Nellie, too," Isabella pipes in.

Nellie smiles. My speaker is on so she can hear them.

"Good night," we all say at the same time.

After I hang up, Nellie says, "Let's get into our sleeping bags. I'm tired, too. Would you mind if I leave my night light on?"

"Not at all," I say. "Great idea."

It feels so warm and soft inside my bag. I'm glad Katrina is in there with me. I think I'm too sleepy to have any spooky dreams. I really hope so.

Chapter 8

★

Here goes nothing!

After my practice sleepover at Nellie's, I'm a little less worried about the party at Brittany's. I made it through the night without waking up. Once I'd had a good night's sleep, I felt happy to be at Nellie's. I might really be ready for a proper sleepover. Still, I hope nobody wants to tell spooky stories.

On the afternoon of the party, Mum helps me wrap my present for Brittany, and I pack my candy cane pyjamas, pillow, and toothbrush in my sleeping bag. Mum says I can take her phone again.

When it's time to go, I give everyone a big hug. Dad carries my sleeping bag out to the car, and I bring Brittany's present.

Now I feel nervous again. What if I'm the first one to arrive at Brittany's? What if I'm the last? Should I have worn a party dress instead of leggings and a snowflake sweater? Will the other girls think my candy cane pyjamas are silly? I forgot to ask Nellie if she was bringing her matching pyjamas.

By the time Dad pulls up to the curb in front of Brittany's house, I feel like telling him to turn the car around and take me back home. Instead, I take a deep breath and get out of the car.

Dad walks me to the door, and I ring the bell.

"Hi, Estella," Brittany says as she swings the door open. She's wearing leggings and a top with a butterfly on it, so I think my outfit is just right. Phew!

Dad carries my sleeping bag in, says hello to Brittany's parents, and gives me a kiss on the head before he leaves.

Ashley and Grace are already here, and Nellie and Alexis come just after Dad leaves. I think I've timed it just right.

We put our sleeping bags on the living room floor, and our presents on the coffee table. Brittany's mum is putting pizza and salad on the kitchen table, and her dad is bringing in art materials.

"Happy Birthday!" I tell Brittany. She's wearing an awesome birthday tiara, and her long brown hair is straight and shiny and pulled up in a pony tail.

"Thanks, Estella," she says, smiling.

"Are those your paintings?" I ask. Along the kitchen wall are a row of square canvasses. Each one is a painting of a monarch butterfly. The first one is simple, like Carlos would paint. Each one is a bit more complicated.

"Yes," says Brittany. "I did the first one when I was three, and one every year after. Dad's a lepidopterist – that's a butterfly scientist – and Mum's an artist, so they helped."

"Wow! What a nice idea," I say. I walk along to look more closely at each one.

"Cool," says Nellie.

"Super-pretty," say Grace and Ashley.

"My mum's are over there." Brittany points to the opposite side of the room.

We all turn to look. The wall is covered with more paintings of monarchs. Some are so detailed they look like photos and others just look like shapes of monarch colours.

"They're beautiful." Alexis moves closer to look. "Are they oil?"

"Thank you." Mrs Lewis smiles. "Yes, they're oil."

"The abstracts are so interesting!" Alexis says.

Nellie and I look at each other and raise our eyebrows.

"Who knew Alexis could give a compliment? And recognize types of paint?" I whisper to Nellie.

"She's just showing off," Nellie whispers back. "And trying to make Brittany's mum like her."

"Or maybe she's being nice," I suggest.

Nellie frowns at me and starts to say something, but she stops when Brittany's dad comes in and puts a pile of paper party plates on the table.

"Dinner is served." He waves one arm out to the side and bows. Then he pulls out our chairs for us.

Ashley sits down on one side of Brittany, and Nellie sits down on the other, so I take a seat across the table between Grace and Alexis. As we eat, Ashley asks Brittany about a book they've both been reading, and Nellie joins in.

Here they go again. Another conversation about a book I haven't read.

But then Brittany says, "Guess what, Estella and Grace? I'm having ballet lessons for my birthday! Mum signed me up this afternoon at the Beach Street School of Dance."

"Are you going to be in our class?" I ask.

"Yes." Brittany nods. "I went to dance classes before we moved, and I really miss it."

"We're getting ready for a recital," says Grace. "Estella and I can help you learn the dance."

"Cool." Brittany smiles.

When we finish eating, Mr Lewis walks around and picks up our paper plates and plastic forks. "I'll do the dishes," he says. He winks, then throws everything into the bin. We all laugh.

Next, Mrs Lewis puts a butterfly-shaped cake in the middle of the table. Mr Lewis brings in the presents and switches off the lights. We sing happy birthday. Then Brittany blows out the candles, and we all clap.

After that, Brittany opens her presents. New books from Nellie and Ashley, a pink purse from Grace, and art stuff from Alexis and me.

"I thought about getting you a book," says Alexis, "but I decided you like art more, since you're having an art party instead of a bookworm party."

Nellie looks at me and rolls her eyes.

Brittany says, "Thank you. I love all of my gifts. I think they're perfect."

Brittany has such good manners it's like she was born to be a princess. My best friend Nellie, not so much. She's being a bit mean about Alexis. It worries me but I don't say anything to her.

"I have something for you, too." Brittany passes out little jars of red and orange lip gloss. The lids are decorated with a monarch butterfly. So pretty! And the lip gloss feels great and smells like oranges.

We eat cake, and then it's time for the art project. Oh, no! After seeing Brittany and Mrs Lewis's art, I don't think I'm going to be able to do this.

We each get a white pillowcase. Mrs Lewis shows us how to put a sheet of cardboard inside so the fabric markers won't soak through to the back. Then she passes out butterfly templates that we can trace with the markers. There's a sample picture to show how to colour it in.

I get to work and use red, orange, and black markers to make my butterfly. Mr Lewis puts on music from one of the princess movies, and we sing and talk as we work.

When I've almost finished, I look up to see the other girls' butterflies. Since we all used the same template, our butterflies look the same. But each one is different, too. Some have lots of little details, others are simpler. But guess what? They all look really pretty. Even mine!

Chapter 9

Best friends forever

Mrs Lewis says we should put on our pyjamas before we watch the movie. I pull mine from my sleeping bag and go into Brittany's room with the other girls.

"Did you get a scary movie?" Ashley asks Brittany as we change into our pyjamas.

"I got the princess movie," says Brittany.

"Oh, not that!" says Alexis. "We've all seen it so many times."

"I love that movie," I tell Brittany. "I don't mind watching it again."

"Me, too," says Grace.

"I'm tired of the princess movie," says Nellie.

"I also have the new movie from our mystery series," says Brittany. "Should we vote?"

"I vote for the mystery movie," says Ashley.

"Me, too," says Nellie.

"I'd rather watch the princess movie," says Grace.

"Me, too," I say.

"Definitely the mystery movie," says Alexis.

"That's two for the princess movie, and three for the mystery movie," says Brittany.

"But you didn't vote," I say.

"I'm not a guest," says Brittany. "Guests get to decide."

"You *are* the birthday girl," says Grace.

"You heard her," says Nellie. "We're going to watch the mystery movie."

"Blimey," I say to Grace. "It seems like the bookworms are ganging up on us."

"It was a vote, fair and square," says Nellie, looking

at me as if she might be angry at me. "And why are you calling us bookworms?"

I fold my arms across my chest and glare at Nellie.

Ashley says, "Nellie's right. It was a fair vote."

"Come on, Ashley," says Nellie. She links her arm through Ashley's.

As they pass, I glare back at Nellie. Then I says, "Let's go, Grace." I link my arm through Grace's.

We sit on top of our sleeping bags on the living room floor and Brittany starts the movie. Nellie's sleeping bag is in between Ashley and Brittany. Mine is in between Grace and Alexis.

I rub my eyes and take a deep breath. I wish it were time to go home. How did everything get so mixed up? I didn't mean to have a fight with Nellie! What happened? We never fight.

I blink back tears and try my best to concentrate on the movie, but I can't. Why is Nellie being so mean? Why am I? And why did I even come to this stupid party?

I really, really want to go home right now. I reach down into my sleeping bag, pull out Mum's phone and slip into the hallway. I'm about to phone her when Nellie comes around the corner.

"Estella," she whispers. "I couldn't find you." She looks like she's about to cry. "What are you doing?"

"I'm calling Mum." I can't stop a tear from sliding down my cheek. "I want to go home."

"So do I." Nellie sniffs. "I want to sleep in my own bed."

"I thought you were grown-up enough for sleepovers now." It's hard to talk and cry at the same time. My voice is sort of squeaking. "What about all that practice with your grandparents?"

"It's not the same." Nellie's crying now, too.

I'm mad at Nellie and at myself. But seeing Nellie so upset makes me want to be brave for both of us. I decide it's time to tell Nellie the truth about how I'm feeling.

I take a deep breath. "I have a big worry that I need to tell you. I think it's why we're having this awful fight."

"What is it?" Nellie sniffs and wipes away a tear.

"I'm worried that you're becoming good friends with Brittany. And Ashley. Because they're in the same class as you," I say. "And they're good readers. And in the top maths group. And I'm not." I take a deep breath. "And I'm worried that you and I won't be best friends any more."

"Really?" Nellie opens her eyes wide. "That's crazy. Because I've been worrying about the same thing! I mean – I've been worrying that you don't need me for a friend any more. Because you and Grace go to dance classes together. And now Brittany will too. And you like the same movies and TV shows."

"No way. I'll always be your best friend," I say.

"Me too," says Nellie. "I like that you're different from me. I'm good at some things, like school stuff, and you're good at other things, like dancing and movies and fashion. And you're nice to people. And you're way more fun than I am. I'm too serious."

I laugh at this. "I'm sorry I called you a bookworm like it was a bad thing. It's awesome that you're a bookworm."

"I'm sorry I made you listen to that spooky story at our practice sleepover. I knew you didn't want to. I didn't really want to, either." Nellie sniffs again. "Should we call our mums to come and get us?"

"I think we should stay," I say.

"What!" says Nellie. "Really?"

"I worked so hard on my times tables to be able to come. It seems like a waste not to stay," I reply.

"That's true," Nellie agrees.

"And Brittany might feel bad if she thinks we're not having fun," I add. "And we *are* Worry Warriors. We're supposed to face our fears."

Nellie smiles. "I suppose a princess would find the courage to stay."

I smile, too. "We can do this! Look – we even have on our matching pyjamas."

"That's because," says Nellie, "when I was getting ready, I asked myself, *What would Estella wear?* And then I wore the same thing."

"Best friends forever?" I ask.

"Best friends forever!" says Nellie.

We give each other a BFF hug, and then call our families to say goodnight.

Chapter 10

Funnest party ever

When Nellie and I go back to the living room, Grace is showing Brittany how to do the dance for our recital. Ashley and Alexis are following along.

"Where did you go?" asks Ashley. "We paused the movie so you wouldn't miss it."

"We just had to make a phone call," I say.

"Come and dance with us!" says Grace.

"We're too sleepy," Nellie and I say at the same time.

Nellie drags her sleeping bag next to mine.

I pull out my pillow and climb in. It feels good.

Nellie gets into her sleeping bag, and we lie on our backs and watch the other girls dance.

"Estella," says Nellie. "Why didn't you tell me you were worried about all that stuff?"

"I don't know," I say. "I didn't want to say anything mean. Mum and Dad's rule is that if you can't say something nice, don't say anything at all."

"I think that's a good rule most of the time," says Nellie. "But I think it's important to tell your best friend if something is bothering you."

"I think you're right. What's that lump?" I cry out. I feel something near my foot in the bottom of my sleeping bag. I reach down and pull out Katrina, my soft ballet doll.

Nellie laughs. "Looks like Sofia helped you pack."

I laugh too. "I don't care if it's babyish. I'm glad Katrina's here."

"I've got a secret in the bottom of my sleeping bag, too." Nellie reaches down and pulls out a big torch. "Just in case."

We laugh again.

My eyelids feel heavy. I'm super-sleepy. I watch the other girls trying to follow Grace as she shows them the dance. She's good, but it's not that easy.

Ashley is having trouble. So is Alexis. Brittany is a good dancer, though. She learns fast.

"That's enough dancing." Ashley turns to Brittany. "Let's tell spooky stories."

"Okay," Brittany nods. "You go first."

The other girls get into their sleeping bags. Brittany turns out the lights and gets into her sleeping bag.

"Once upon a time," Ashley uses a spooky voice, "there was a boy who was good at carving animals out of wood. One night he carved a monkey."

Nellie pokes my arm, and I poke her back. Ashley must have found the same book of scary stories that Nellie's got!

"The good thing," I whisper, "is that this story isn't so scary when you've already heard it."

Nellie nods and smiles.

"Maybe we should stop," says Grace, when Ashley gets to the part with thunder and lightning. "I'm getting a bit spooked."

"It is quite scary," agrees Brittany.

"Let's talk about the princess movie," says Grace. "Does anyone else have relatives who might come and tell them they're heir to the throne?"

"That's silly, Grace," says Alexis. "The girl in the movie never knew her father. If any of us were in line to be princess, our mums or dads would have told us."

"Oh, that's true," says Grace. "I never thought of that."

"Let's watch the rest of the mystery movie," says Ashley.

"Good idea," we all say. Brittany starts it again from the beginning.

This time I can enjoy the movie. Even though there are no princesses, mermaids, or dancing, it's a good story. It takes place in Paris. It's about a ten-year-old boy who's a good painter, and after he paints a scene, he can walk into

the canvas. Then he's in a different time and place! While he's there, he solves a mystery.

"That was so good," I tell Brittany when it's over.

"The book is even better," says Brittany. "And in each book in the series, he goes to a different time and place."

"Read us the beginning of the next book," Alexis says to Brittany.

"Okay." Brittany pulls the book from her pile of birthday presents and opens to the first page. Nellie offers Brittany her torch.

It's warm and soft inside my sleeping bag. I hug Katrina as I listen to Brittany read. She has a good voice. And the mystery book is really good. Maybe I'll borrow this one from Nellie and finish reading it on my own.

As I snuggle down into my sleeping bag, I think about how worried I was about sleeping over. Was it worth all that time to practise my maths times tables so I could come? I decide it was. I was really proud to get every question right on my test. And even though Nellie will always be my *best* friend, it's fun to spend time with other friends. Maybe we're growing up a little. But not too much!

I think about what Alexis said – that it's silly to think I might be long-lost heir to the throne. I guess I always knew that, but it's fun to pretend. I'm still going to practise my princess skills.

Just before I fall asleep, I have the best idea ever. If my long-lost relatives show up to tell me I'm royalty before my next birthday, I'm going to have a princess sleepover party in the castle.

ABOUT THE AUTHOR

Marne Ventura is the author of twenty-nine children's books, ten of them for Capstone. A former primary school teacher, she holds a master's degree in education from the University of California. When she's not writing, she enjoys arts and crafts, cooking and baking, and spending time with her family. Marne lives with her husband on the central coast of California. This is her first venture into fiction.

ABOUT THE ILLUSTRATOR

Leo Trinidad is an illustrator and animator who has created many animated characters and television shows for companies including Disney and Dreamworks, but his great passion is illustrating children's books. Leo graduated with honours from the Veritas University of Arts and Design in San Jose, Costa Rica, where he lives with his wife and daughter. Visit him online at www.leotrinidad.com

GLOSSARY

arabesque ballet move where the dancer stands on one leg and extends the other behind

architect person who designs buildings and advises in their construction

assistant someone who helps a leader with a project

bookworm someone who loves books and spends a lot of time reading

catastrophe large disaster

compliment remark or action that shows you appreciate something

heir someone who has, or will be, left a title, property, or money

optional something that you can, but don't have to, do

recital show where people dance, sing or play a musical instrument for others

template pattern used to draw or cut around to make the same shape in another material

tradition custom, idea, or belief passed down through time

Vikings group of Scandinavian warriors who raided other European countries in the 8th to 10th century

TALK ABOUT IT

1. Estella was very nervous about not doing well in maths. She asked her friends for help. What would you have done in her place?

2. Estella is worried that she is going to lose her best friend now that they are in different classes. Have you ever drifted apart from a good friend?

3. Estella wants more than anything else to be a princess. Is there anything you would really like to be or do? How would you go about making that happen?

WRITE ABOUT IT

1. Think about a time you were worried about something. Write about how you felt and what you did to feel better.

2. Who is your favourite character in this story? Draw a picture of that person. Then write a list of five things you like about them.

3. How would you have helped Estella with her worry? Think about that, and then write down what you would have done.

DON'T WORRY! THERE ARE MORE Worry WARRIORS

READ THEM ALL!

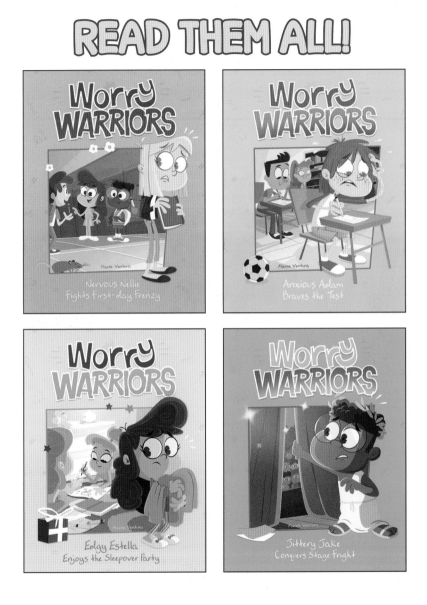